An Adams' Wood Mystery

WHO SPILLED THE PAINT?

Follow the clues and find the answer

Written by Stewart Cowley
Illustrated by Susi Adams

DERRYDALE BOOKS
NEW YORK

Published 1986 by Derrydale Books,
distributed by Crown Publishers, Inc.

Produced for Derrydale Books by
Victoria House Publishing Ltd.
4/5 Lower Borough Walls
Bath BA1 1QR, England

Printed in Belgium

Welcome to Adams' Wood

"Hello, I'm Holmes Mouse, the great detective!"

"And I'm Watson Mouse, his best friend!"

This is a story about a concert given by our friends in the woods, and the day they built a beautiful new bandstand. But who do you think spilled paint all over it? Will you help us find out?

Read the story and look at the pictures carefully to find the clues. We will be looking for clues, too—watch out for us.

If you don't solve the mystery, we've put together all the evidence in one big picture near the end of the book ... and if you still don't know who spilled the paint, we may have found the answer for you.

It was concert day in Adams' Wood. Mr. Fox was going to conduct the band, and everyone was looking forward to hearing the beautiful music.

Mr. Beaver the builder had drawn up plans for a lovely new bandstand. It was his job to tell his helpers exactly what to do.

Billy had a very important job. He was cutting all the wood to just the right size.

"Careful, Billy! Don't cut yourself."

The little rabbits were going to help with the painting. Mrs. Rabbit had brought them boots and overalls, but none of them were the right size! "Oh dear," she said. "Well, children, never mind, they'll have to do!"

"You are clumsy, Bobtail!"

Bobtail was helping Mr. Squirrel, who was sorting out the wood for Billy to cut. "Careful, Bobtail," he called. But it was too late. Bobtail tripped over his boots and knocked over all the wood!

"Make sure you don't knock over the bandstand,"
laughed Sammy. He was good at climbing, so he was in
charge of making the flagpole on top of the roof.

Mr. Raccoon was in charge of setting up the chairs for everyone to sit on. But what a terrible muddle he was getting into!

Mr. Rabbit was hurrying along with the programs. He was very pleased because Bobtail was the first to play.

"Oh no!" called Miss Mouse. "Someone has spilled bright red paint all over the new steps. What a mess! And they've tracked it everywhere with their great big feet. Who could have done it?"

"Who do we know with big feet?"

"It wasn't us," cried the little mice.
"We've been practicing our singing.
Listen!" And they all took a deep breath
and burst into song.

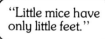

"Little mice have only little feet."

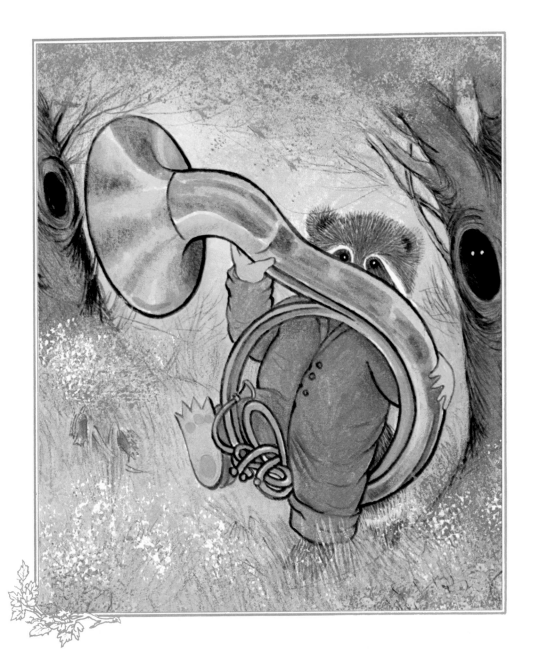

Robbie Raccoon was all tangled up in a tuba. "I must practice my piece," he puffed. "Only I can't find the right end to blow into. I wish I was playing the trumpet like Bobtail."

"Whoever stepped in all that paint has knocked over the music stands. He must have been in a hurry!" said Mrs. Hedgehog.

"There are those big red footprints again."

"Oh dear! Who was going to play first?"

Mr. Frog had put all the sheet music in order, but now it was scattered everywhere! "There are red fingerprints all over the music," he said. "And the first sheet is missing!"

Mrs. Fox was tuning her violin. "I didn't see anybody," she said. "But I can hear somebody. Listen!"
Someone hidden in the bushes was playing a trumpet.

"Now we know who spilled the paint. Do you? Turn the page and see who it is."

You and your big boots have made a real mess, Bobtail.
But you're playing your trumpet beautifully!